THE TIMEKEEPERS

First Flight

Contents

Chapter 1

Flying back in time

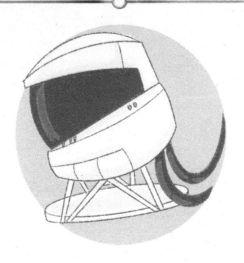

Yasmin battled to hold the joystick straight. The wind was pushing hard, and visibility was bad. Rain lashed across the windshield as she fought to keep the plane under control. There was the runway! She could do this. Putting both hands on the joystick she eased it away

from her. The nose of the plane smoothly
dipped down. The ground was coming
closer… closer… She felt a gentle bump
as the wheels touched down. It was a
perfect landing! Smiling to herself, Yasmin
took off her headset and shook out her
hair. She had always wanted to fly, and
now she had.

Well, almost. This was just a flight simulator at an air show near her home in Karachi, Pakistan, and she hadn't really been battling the elements. But it felt like she had, and that's what counted. *One day I'll do it for real,* she thought to herself as she opened the flight simulator door.

"How did that feel?" asked her mum, as Yasmin joined her parents.

"Amazing," said Yasmin honestly. "I could do it all day."

Her dad smiled and took her hand. "There are some wonderful planes here, Yasmin. You're going to love it! We've just got time to see some exhibits before the air display."

There were planes on display from the whole history of human flight. They stood proudly around the hangar, with big signs that told the visitors all about them. There was a British Spitfire from World War II, and one of the earliest jet aeroplanes. There were biplanes with their two sets of wings, and a great bulky bomber painted with camouflage. Yasmin ran among them, reading about their histories and imagining herself behind the controls, up in the sky.

She stopped at a replica of the first plane to make a powered, piloted flight – the Wright Flyer, built by Orville and Wilbur Wright in 1903. Yasmin closed her eyes and imagined how it must have felt, to be the first people in the world to make a flight like that! Not gliding, but real, actual *flying*.

She suddenly felt a whirring on her wrist. She glanced down at her special Timekeepers watch. The hands had started to spin – *backwards*. Yasmin felt a rush of excitement. She was being called to the History Hub!

Yasmin had a wonderful secret. *She could travel back in time.* She was one of the Timekeepers – a secret organisation that kept the course of history on track! They had the best fun, travelling into the past and making sure that everything happened the way it was supposed to. But they always had to watch out for a villain called DeLay, who liked messing around with history a little too much…

Yasmin felt worried as well as excited as she gazed at her watch. The Timekeepers were only summoned when DeLay was causing trouble. They were the only ones who could stop him! What was he up to now?

She flipped up the watch face to reveal a hidden screen of buttons. Then she glanced over at her parents, who were reading the information beside an old seaplane. Time wouldn't move while she was away, so her parents wouldn't be worried. But it was good to know that they were enjoying themselves right now.

Yasmin took a deep breath and touched a button on the watch. The hands spun faster. Everything around her stopped, so Yasmin felt as if she was inside a photograph. There was a whirl of rainbow colours as her feet lifted off the ground. Then everything went white.

Yasmin blinked and shook her head. She was standing in a large museum, crammed from floor to ceiling with objects from throughout history, from early flint tools to modern smartphones. This was the History Hub: the Timekeepers' HQ.

"Yasmin, here!" she said. She headed over to her favourite section of the museum to wait for the others. *Coding has come a loooong way,* she thought, as she gazed at the boxy computer screens and heavy keyboards on display.

"Cuckoo! Cuckoo!"
squawked a familiar voice.

Yasmin glanced up at
the large clock on the wall.
It had a swinging pendulum and was
decorated like a gingerbread house.
Just above the clock face, there was a
door – and out of the door peeped
a little bird, sitting on a comfy nest.

Yasmin smiled. "Hi, Tempo!"

Tempo ruffled her striped feathers.
"Cuckoo!" she said again.

Flashes of light began to appear
all around Yasmin as the other
Timekeepers arrived.

"Luke, here!" called a tall boy in a
beautiful handmade poncho. Luke loved
fashion. Yasmin never knew what he

would be wearing from one mission to the next!

A girl in paint-spattered overalls appeared. "Hannah, here!" Hannah was the Timekeepers' art expert.

"Jackson, here!" A boy arrived in a cloud of white flour, waving his hand and coughing a little. He was still wearing his baking apron.

"Sarah, here!" Sarah was a girl whose pockets bristled with pens and notebooks. She knew about the authors and poets of the past.

"Rosa, here!" Rosa wiped her hands down her brightly coloured football kit. From the look of her she had been in the middle of a match!

A boy adjusted the guitar slung over his shoulder and smiled amiably at the others. "Kingsley, here!"

"Min-Jun, here – and sticky!" Min-Jun declared,

gingerly holding his latest model between two fingers: a freshly glued plane.

The Timekeepers gathered around the display case in the centre of the museum. Whatever appeared inside would give them a clue about their next adventure. *What will it be today?* Yasmin wondered. *And which two Timekeepers will the History Hub choose for the mission?*

A little ball of light began to grow inside the display case and an object appeared. It looked like…

"Is that a weather vane?" asked Yasmin.

"Maybe?" said Min Jun.

"Whatever it is, it's going to help us beat DeLay," said Luke, and the others all murmured in agreement.

There was a fluttering of wings. Yasmin felt the light brush of Tempo's feathers as the cuckoo settled briefly on her shoulder.

"Yes!" she cried. "I'm on this mission. Who's with me?"

Tempo fluttered up and swooped around a couple of times before landing a little clumsily on Min-Jun's head.

"Me, by the look of things," said Min-Jun, laughing as he peered up through his fringe.

"Cuckoo!" said Tempo.

The little bird jumped off Min-Jun and flew towards the display case, where she settled and started preening her feathers.

Yasmin opened the display-case door and carefully took out the strange object. It did look like a weather vane, with a long stem topped with four cups, tilted sideways to catch the wind. But Yasmin knew from experience that things weren't always as they seemed. She put the object in her backpack.

Tempo flew on to Yasmin's shoulder. She always accompanied the Timekeepers on their missions. "Cuckoo!" she squawked with excitement.

"Good to have you with us, Tempo," said Min-Jun with a grin.

"We can always use a helping wing!" Yasmin joked.

"Cuckoo!" said Tempo cheerfully.

The other Timekeepers opened their watches to reveal six screens, ready to help Yasmin and Min-Jun if they needed it. Tempo began to fly around Yasmin and Min-Jun, faster and faster, until the stripes on her feathers blurred into wide, sweeping circles. Light burst around them.

FLASH!

Yasmin blinked away the last dancing spots of light. The first thing she noticed was the fresh, clean smell of the sea, and the roar of waves crashing against a sandy shore. She looked down at her long brown skirt and neatly pinned blue blouse. She had a hat on her head, and stout leather boots on her feet.

Min-Jun was wearing trousers, a light-coloured shirt, and a waistcoat. He pushed the checked woollen cap back off his head and grinned at Yasmin. "Great outfit," he said. "When are we?"

"Cuckoo!" said Tempo, still perched on Yasmin's shoulder.

Yasmin checked her watch. "It's 1903, and we're on a beach in Kitty Hawk, in North Carolina, USA," she said slowly. "Hey! That's where the Wright brothers flew their first—"

"Watch out!" Min-Jun suddenly shouted.

Yasmin looked up from her watch. A plane was skidding across the sand, heading right towards them!

Chapter 2

"Tarnation!"

Clouds of sand whirled in the air as the plane thundered towards them. Yasmin and Min-Jun were deafened by the roar of an enormous propeller. They threw themselves out of the way just in time. It was hard in these old-fashioned clothes, and Yasmin's skirt tangled around her legs

as she scrambled up a nearby sand dune.
Min-Jun was close behind her. He had
lost his hat.

"Cuckoo!" shouted Tempo in alarm.
"Cuckoo! Cuckoo!"

With a final sputtering sound from the propeller, everything fell quiet. The dust and sand settled. Yasmin and Min-Jun sank on to the dune and stared at the amazing machine in front of them.

It looked nothing like a modern plane. It had a wooden framework that reminded Yasmin of Min-Jun's model, and two sets of wide canvas wings, one on top of the other, separated by rows of wooden struts. There were two large wooden propellers, and what looked like a small engine fixed above the pilot. The pilot wasn't seated, like Yasmin had expected, but lying down on his front.

"Tarnation!" the pilot cried in disappointment. Clearly the flight hadn't gone to plan.

"I was *going* to say," Yasmin told Min-Jun as she caught her breath, "that Kitty Hawk is where the Wright brothers made the first ever powered flight, in 1903."

"Awesome!" said Min-Jun, looking
at the plane on the sand in front of them
with admiration.

"Cuckoo," said Tempo, looking a
bit ruffled.

"Wilbur! Hey, Wilbur!" Another man
came running towards the plane, his scarf
flying behind him. "Did the attempt
damage the plane?"

"You're more worried about the Flyer than about me, Orville," said the pilot a little grumpily. "I'm doing just fine, thanks for asking."

Yasmin wanted to shout with excitement. It was the Wright brothers themselves!

It looked like Wilbur was struggling to take off his harness. Yasmin and Min-Jun ran down the dune to offer help.

"I'm sorry for almost hitting you there," apologised the pilot as he finally wriggled out of his seat and dropped down on to the sand. "You appeared out of nowhere! How do you do? I'm Wilbur Wright, and that's my brother, Orville."

Orville Wright had reached the plane. He breathlessly tipped his bowler hat at Yasmin and Min-Jun. "Thanks for your help, uh…?"

Yasmin and Min-Jun introduced themselves. Min-Jun had found his hat at the bottom of the dune, and tipped it politely the way Orville Wright had done.

"We're just, ah, visiting this beach today," Min-Jun said. That much was true, at least!

"Well, we hope you don't think too badly of the place," said Wilbur as he dusted sand off his waistcoat.

"What's wrong with your—"Yasmin began. Just in time she remembered that nobody in 1903 would know what the Flyer was. Even the word 'plane' would be wrong. "…machine?" she finished.

"Darned if I know," confessed Wilbur.

Orville scratched his head as he and his brother looked the Flyer over.

"Rudder's in the wrong position, I reckon," said Orville finally.

Wilbur's expression cleared. "No wonder it wouldn't take off. One of the propellers stopped working mid-flight, too.

Just the strangest thing. One minute it was turning, the next minute – nothing."

They all jumped as a whirring sound started up from the grounded plane. A propeller had started turning, as if it had heard Wilbur talking about it. The Wright brothers stared.

"Will you look at that!" said Orville in surprise.

Yasmin and Min-Jun shared a look. Things stopping and starting again for no reason? That sounded like a Time Crunch – a moment when time froze, or repeated, or fast-forwarded. There was only one person who used Time Crunches to cause this kind of mischief. DeLay! The arch time villain was somewhere nearby…

"We need to get the Flyer back to the hangar," Orville was saying to his brother.

"Need some help?" offered Min-Jun.

Yasmin and Min-Jun helped Orville and Wilbur tow the Flyer back up the beach. It was pretty light for an aircraft, but it was still hard work. Yasmin and Min-Jun had to stop a few times to wipe their foreheads. Tempo flew overhead, calling, "Cuckoo! Cuckoo!" in encouragement.

"Nice bird," said Orville, shading his eyes as he looked up at Tempo swooping and circling.

"Studying how birds fly has really helped us build our flying machines," said Wilbur. "See how your bird uses her wings?"

Yasmin gazed at the way Tempo tilted her wings to catch the ocean breeze. There were no trees for miles in Kitty Hawk, and the steady north to north-east winds consistently sweeping the beach made it a great place for the Wright brothers' flying attempts. She nodded.

"Same thing with the Flyer," said Wilbur proudly, patting the machine. "Our first experiments were with gliders up in the old lighthouse. Then we added an engine, to see if we could get moving with something more than just the power of the wind. We're making progress."

"We think the Flyer might be the one," Orville added. "Once we sort out the rudder."

They reached the Wrights' hangar
and helped carry the Flyer inside. Yasmin
gazed around at the wide open space,
with the smaller workshop to one side.
There were clamps and saws, wrenches,
and scattered pieces of timber; rolls of
canvas fabric, and engine parts scattered
on tabletops. There was even a glider,
lying quietly on its side with one fabric-
covered wing tilted towards the roof.

"Pass me a wrench, Wilbur," said
Orville, holding out a hand. "I need to
take a closer look at that rudder."

Yasmin and Min-Jun sat on a bench that stood against the wall of the hangar and watched the Wright brothers at work. Tempo found a comfortable perch in the rafters and happily shouted, "Cuckoo!" every few minutes.

"Hey," said Orville suddenly, wriggling out from beneath the Flyer. "What time's the supply boat due in?"

Wilbur glanced at a large clock on the rough wooden wall. "Any minute," he said. "Reckon we'll be late if we don't go right away."

Yasmin exchanged a glance with Min-Jun. This was a great opportunity to start looking for DeLay! She jumped up. "Can we help?"

"Could you go meet the boat?" said Wilbur. He wiped his face with the back of his hand, leaving a smear of oil on his forehead. "If we don't pick up our supplies, we'll be pretty stuck. It would be very kind of you."

Yasmin was surprised. She thought Kitty Hawk had a bridge to the mainland. Why did the Wrights need a boat? Then she realised the bridge hadn't been built in 1903.

"Where does the boat come in?" Min-Jun asked.

"A couple of miles down the beach," said Orville. "Take our bicycles, if you want. Do you ride?"

Yasmin and Min-Jun both nodded.

"We made them ourselves," said
Wilbur with pride, showing them two
bicycles propped up outside the hangar.
"We had a bike shop, back in Ohio. Our
sister Katherine still runs that."

"We designed the Flyer with these in mind, as well as birds," said Orville. He patted Yasmin's handlebars. "The Flyer leans and banks, just the same as our bicycles."

"Cool," said Min-Jun.

Wilbur frowned. "Yes, I suppose the wind is a little chilly."

"But once you start cycling, you'll soon warm up!" added Orville.

Yasmin stifled a giggle. The Wrights thought Min-Jun was talking about the weather!

She and Min-Jun cycled away down the beach to fetch the supplies with Tempo flying overhead. DeLay was around here somewhere. It was time to track him down…

Chapter 3

Time Crunch

The bicycles were heavier and bumpier than Yasmin and Min-Jun were used to. They didn't have modern bicycle suspensions to cushion them as they rattled along. There were no gears either, so it was hard work. But the machinery was well-oiled and the pedals turned easily. They cycled down a wooden boardwalk, passing beaches and dunes.

"Cuckoo!" Tempo swooped happily over their heads, enjoying the ocean wind beneath her wings.

A lighthouse stood in the distance, black and white, looking out to sea. To Yasmin's delight, there were herds of wild horses grazing among the dune grasses and galloping along the sand. And all the while, a breeze was blowing in from the Atlantic Ocean, keeping them 'cool'.

She was having so much
fun that she almost forgot to
keep an eye out for DeLay.
Watching Tempo glide and soar reminded
her of their mission – if they didn't stop
the villain, the Wright Brothers wouldn't
make their first successful flight...

By the time they reached the supply
boat, which had docked at a wide
wooden jetty, they still hadn't spotted any
sign of DeLay.

"We're here for the Wright Brothers'
supplies" said Min-Jun breathlessly.

Two boxes were loaded on to the
back of the bicycles. Yasmin suppressed a
small groan at the thought of cycling
back again. The bicycles were even
heavier now!

"Cuckoo!" Tempo chirped in encouragement as they set off.

"Easy for you to say!" said Min-Jun, huffing and puffing.

By the time they arrived back at the hangar, their cheeks glowed. "Good old Katherine!" exclaimed Wilbur as the brothers eagerly unpacked the boxes. There was flour, and apples, a can of oil, several tins of beans, a packet of letters, and even a bag of orange and yellow sweets. "I don't know where we'd be without her!"

"Want some candy?" Orville offered, holding out the sweets.

"We couldn't manage without our sister," said Wilbur. "We already told you she keeps our bicycle shop running back in Ohio, right?"

"And more besides," said Orville. "She's wonderful at telling people about our work, and keeping us organised."

"I've heard of Katherine Wright," Yasmin whispered to Min-Jun as they leaned against the wall of the hangar, munching on the candy. "She travelled all over the world with her brothers, representing the Wright company."

"Does your bird like apples?" asked Wilbur. He cut a slice off an apple and offered it to Tempo.

Tempo fluttered down from her perch in the rafters and took the apple slice. But then…

"Cuckoo!" she cried, spitting out the treat. "Cuckoo, cuckoo!"

"What…?" said Wilbur.

They all gazed at the apple slice lying on the floor. The edges were curling up as they watched. The once-crisp apple flesh shrivelled and developed spots of blue mould. It was rotting away, right before their eyes.

Yasmin swung around and stared at the rest of the supplies.

The bag of flour had collapsed, with a bloom of green mould developing around the bottom. The tins of beans were rusting, bending… breaking open right in front of her. She caught Min-Jun's eye. This was bad. DeLay was here, messing around with his Time Crunches again and changing how time works. He might even be inside the hangar itself, causing mischief with the planes!

The Wrights were still staring at the rotten apple.

"Can you please show us your flying machines?" Min-Jun blurted, before Orville and Wilbur could turn around and

see the mess that DeLay had made with the rest of the supplies.

The frown on Orville's face cleared. He smiled at Min-Jun and Yasmin. "Sure! Follow me."

They left the workshop and entered the yawning space of the hangar. Everything was quiet. Dust danced in the air, and there were little heaps of sand in the corners, blown in from Kitty Hawk beach.

"Wilbur fixed the rudder," Orville said proudly as they approached the Flyer, which stood by itself near the entrance to the hangar. "I reckon we'll get the Flyer in the air the next time the wind is right."

Yasmin and Min-Jun looked at the Flyer. There was a feeling of unease in Yasmin's belly. Something was different, she thought with a frown. She couldn't put her finger on it, but it looked – slightly lopsided.

Wilbur gave a sharp cry of dismay. "Where's the second propeller?" he said.

Yasmin's eyes widened. No wonder the Flyer looked lopsided. Instead of two propellers – one on each side of the pilot's seat – there was only one!

DeLay was up to his old tricks. He was trying to stop the first powered flight from ever taking place.

Chapter 4

Down with DeLay!

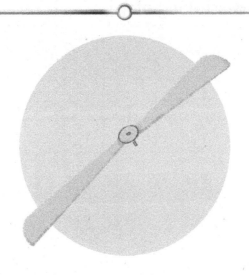

The Wright brothers hunted all over the hangar for the propeller. No luck. Yasmin and Min-Jun felt awful.

"We need that propeller," said Orville.

"Without it, we'll never get the Flyer off the ground!" said Wilbur.

Yasmin and Min-Jun looked at each

other. There was often a moment in the Timekeepers' missions when they had to explain about DeLay without mentioning time travel. Telling people about that could change history, and that was NOT what the Timekeepers were here to do.

"This is going to sound kind of strange," Min-Jun began.

"Stranger than a propeller disappearing into thin air?" said Wilbur.

Taking turns, Min-Jun and Yasmin

explained about DeLay.

"He's a troublemaker," said Yasmin.

"He messes around with people's lives," said Min-Jun.

"And we think he's trying to stop you from flying!" Yasmin finished. "He's the one who stole your propeller. We're sure of it!"

Orville and Wilbur both looked shocked. Orville sank on to a nearby bench with his head in his hands. "This is terrible," he muttered. "Just terrible."

"Maybe it's not so bad," said Min-Jun hopefully. "Can't you just make another one?"

"I wish it was that simple," said Wilbur. "Each propeller is hand-carved. We put so much work into matching the propellers so that the power was evenly distributed. We've carved, and polished, and carved, and polished, and measured, and carved some more. Making sure that our two propellers matched was the hardest thing we've ever done."

"We aren't even sure we have the science right," said Orville sadly. "We're still testing. But we really hoped we'd nailed it this time. We'll never be able to replicate that propeller again."

"And after the failure earlier today, this is the last straw," said Wilbur. He sank down on the bench beside his brother. "Our dream of flying is over. We might as well go back to Ohio and help Katherine sell our bicycles."

Yasmin wanted to yell with frustration. DeLay had stopped the Wrights from conducting the most important experiment in the history of powered flight! Without the success of the Flyer, the world of aviation would never develop. There would be no air show in

Karachi. No flight simulator for Yasmin to explore her own dreams of flying. It was a disaster.

They had to stop DeLay and find that propeller!

"You search the rest of the hangar," Yasmin suggested to Orville and Wilbur. "We'll take a look on the beach."

Yasmin and Min-Jun took the bicycles and pedalled back out into the bright December sunshine. The smell of the sea was rich and salty, and seagulls flew in white circles high in the sky. Tempo swooped around their heads in a worried kind of way.

Yasmin and Min-Jun bumped along the salt-spotted boardwalk, scanning the beach. But apart from the occasional lump of driftwood, there was nothing.

"Cuckoo!" said Tempo suddenly. She flapped her wings extra hard, and soared high into the air. "Cuckoo!"

Yasmin stopped pedalling, resting her feet on the boardwalk. Min-Jun did the same.

"What have you seen, Tempo?" Yasmin asked.

She and Min-Jun stared down the beach. A group of wild horses were gathered by the water's edge. They stood in a tight circle with their heads down, looking curiously at something.

"Come on," said Yasmin, propping up her bicycle against a piece of fencing. "Let's take a look."

They raced together down the soft sand. One of the horses noticed them, tossed its grey head, and whinnied at the others. The horses were all beautiful, with dappled coats and long, salt-tangled manes. As one, they whirled about and galloped away – revealing…

"It's just another piece of driftwood," said Min-Jun in disappointment.

"It looks more like a tree," Yasmin said.

But as they got closer, Yasmin realised that it wasn't a tree at all.

Min-Jun punched the air. "Beaten you already, DeLay!" he said excitedly.

Yasmin couldn't believe DeLay had made it so easy. They were hardly any distance from the hangar – and yet there was no denying it. They were definitely looking at a propeller.

It was easy to see how they had mistaken it for a tree. Someone had stuck it into the ground and tied some branches to the top to disguise it. Yasmin inspected it curiously. She had no idea propellers were so big. This one towered over them, standing a good eight feet high.

Yasmin gave it a tug. It tilted slightly. "Come on Min-Jun, help me!" she said.

They pulled off the fake branches and tugged at the enormous object until it fell flat on to the sand. Just like Wilbur had said, it was carved from a single piece of wood, with a twisting shape designed to catch the wind as it turned. Yasmin took one end and Min-Jun took the other. They had beaten DeLay already! The Wrights would make their famous flight after all – maybe even that very afternoon.

"Down with DeLay," sang Yasmin as she and Min-Jun carried the propeller blade up the beach. "Hey, hey, hey! Down with DeLay!"

"Koo-Koo-cuckoo-koo!" shouted Tempo joyfully from her perch on top of Yasmin's head.

"This must be the fastest Timekeepers mission ever," Min-Jun joked. They balanced the propeller carefully across their bikes, and started pushing it back up the boardwalk.

"You'd think DeLay would come up with a better plan than this!" agreed Yasmin with a grin. "I can't wait to see Wilbur and Orville's faces."

The brothers were waiting anxiously in their workshop. Yasmin and Min-Jun wheeled the propeller proudly into the hangar.

"Ta da!" said Yasmin with a flourish. "One propeller."

"Oh," said Orville.

"Oh no," said Wilbur.

Yasmin exchanged a look of surprise with Min-Jun. This wasn't the reaction they were expecting.

"Is there a problem?" said Min-Jun.

If anything, the brothers looked more defeated than before.

"It's an old propeller," said Wilbur.

"Which didn't work," said Orville.

All the feelings of pride and triumph oozed out of Yasmin. She should have known. Finding it had been way too easy. DeLay must have stolen the old propeller to trick them. They had fallen right into his time-meddling hands.

"Cuckoo," said Tempo sadly. Her feathers looked like they were drooping.

"We hunted all over the hangar, the workshop and the yards outside," said Orville. "There is no sign of it anywhere."

"Thanks for your help," said Wilbur quietly. "But I think it's time my brother and I went back home to Ohio. There's nothing here for us any more."

Chapter 5

A helping wing

"We can't let Orville and Wilbur give up,"
said Yasmin in determination as they
cycled back down the boardwalk. "It's
too important."

"Cuckoo," agreed Tempo, perched on
Yasmin's handlebars. The ocean breeze
was blowing her feathers around, so she

looked more like a mop
than a bird.

"They seem pretty
certain that they couldn't do it
without that propeller," said
Min-Jun gloomily.

"I think it's time to call the others,"
said Yasmin. "They may have
some ideas."

They wheeled their bicycles in among
the sand dunes, to get out of the wind.
Then they laid them down carefully on
the sandy ground, and pushed up their
sleeves. Their special Timekeeper
watches blinked at them. Yasmin and
Min-Jun both flipped them up, and
pressed a button.

The other Timekeepers appeared: a tiny gallery of faces on the screens concealed inside the watches.

"Hey, guys," said Kingsley.

"How's it going?" asked Rosa. She still had a speck of mud on her nose.

"Not great," Yasmin confessed. "DeLay has stolen a propeller from the Wright brothers' plane. We can't find it anywhere. They're talking about giving up and going home to Ohio before they've made the first powered flight in history."

Sarah looked concerned. "You've looked everywhere you can think of?"

"There's too much ground to cover," said Min-Jun. "Kitty Hawk beach is enormous. The propeller could be anywhere. And we've only got a couple of bicycles between us."

"I wish we could borrow a plane to cover a wider area," said Yasmin gloomily. "But we can't borrow a plane which hasn't been invented yet!"

The other Timekeepers looked thoughtful.

Tempo started pecking Yasmin's watch screen. "Cuckoo," she said. She sounded insistent. "Cuckoo, cuckoo!"

"Tempo!" said Sarah suddenly. "That's it!"

"What do you mean?"
asked Min-Jun.

Tempo spread her wings and flapped them vigorously, clinging to Yasmin's arm.

"Humans may not be able to fly yet," Sarah said, "but Tempo can!"

"Cuckoo!" shouted Tempo. *Finally*, she seemed to be saying!

"Of course!" exclaimed Min-Jun.

Yasmin rolled her eyes at herself. They'd had a perfect flying machine all along, and hadn't even realised it!

"Thanks guys," she said gratefully. "You're the best."

The others waved and disappeared. The screens on Yasmin and Min-Jun's watches went dark.

"Looks like this is up to you, Tempo,"

Yasmin said to the little cuckoo perched on her arm. "Fly up as high as you can, and tell us if you see anything!"

"Up," said Min-Jun, pointing helpfully at the mass of clouds in the December sky. "Up!"

Tempo cocked her head. Then she spread her wings and took off, spiralling up into the sky until she was just a stripy dot far above their heads. Down on the sand dunes, Yasmin and Min-Jun exchanged a high-five, hopped back on to their bicycles, and followed her.

Now they just had to hope that the little cuckoo would find the clue they all needed so desperately.

It was difficult to keep track of Tempo as she flew. But every now and then, she swooped down, to check that they were still following. The waves crashed on the shore, sweeping up and down the sand as Yasmin and Min-Jun pedalled along.

Yasmin concentrated on keeping the wheels of her bicycle away from the sand. They were nearing the lighthouse again. She remembered seeing it on their ride to the supply boat.

Tempo fluttered down in a whoosh of striped feathers.

"Anything yet, Tempo?" asked Min-Jun.

"Cuckoo!" said Tempo.

She rocketed right up into the sky again. Yasmin stopped the bike and shaded her eyes to keep track.

"She's heading for the lighthouse," said Min-Jun suddenly.

Sure enough, Yasmin saw Tempo land on the top of the lighthouse.

The little bird stretched out her wings and flapped them urgently. "Cuckoo!" she cried. "Cuckoo!"

"Do you think there's something up there?" Yasmin asked Min-Jun.

Min-Jun had stopped his bike too. He pushed back his hat and squinted at the lighthouse. "She's being pretty loud," he observed.

"CUCKOO!" shouted Tempo. She circled the lighthouse once, twice, three times, and landed again at the very top. "CUCKOO!"

Excitement stirred in Yasmin's belly. "She's definitely seen something," she said, getting back on to her bike.

A path led down from the

74

boardwalk to the lighthouse. It was
narrower than the main route, and a lot
bumpier, so Yasmin and Min-Jun pedalled
carefully. Propping their bicycles against
the weathered wooden lighthouse door,
they tried the handle. The door
creaked open.

The space inside was small and dusty,
with a rickety spiral staircase that curled
up towards the light at the very top. They
could still hear Tempo cuckooing
loudly outside.

The staircase was tight and twisted. Yasmin took the lead, with Min-Jun following up the creaky wooden treads. Yasmin felt quite dizzy by the time they reached the top.

The top of the lighthouse was flooded with light. Yasmin stared at the waves crashing far below, and the wide blue horizon of the Atlantic Ocean. She wondered what it would be like to be up here on a stormy night.

"Look!" Min-Jun shouted.

Yasmin tore her eyes from the view. Lying in the middle of the circular space at the top of the lighthouse was something long and wooden, with a familiar carved and twisted shape. The propeller!

"So you've found it at last," said a
horribly familiar voice.

Yasmin and Min-Jun whirled around.
A tall, bony figure stood at the top of the
lighthouse stairs. He wore a long robe
decorated with hourglasses, which
flapped about him as if caught in a
strong wind. His hair writhed on his head
like a nest of wild white snakes. His eyes
gleamed like flat, wet pebbles.

Yasmin gasped. It was none other
than DeLay himself!

Chapter 6

An escape plan

Time seemed to stand still. Yasmin and
Min-Jun stood frozen and even the waves
outside the lighthouse seemed to fall
silent. Perhaps time really *had* stopped,
Yasmin thought. Stopping time was one
of DeLay's specialities, after all.

The wild-haired villain smiled

mockingly at Yasmin and Min-Jun, and swept a low bow.

"I congratulate you on your persistence," he said. "But you are too late. Even now, those useless brothers are packing up their toys and preparing to head back to Ohio."

"This isn't over yet, DeLay," said Min-Jun fiercely. "We're taking this propeller back, and you can't stop us!"

Tempo zoomed around DeLay's head, squawking furiously.

"Get your little bird under control," said DeLay, scowling. "No one likes a bad loser. There's nothing you can do to stop me this time. TIME! Ha!"

He scooped up the propeller. Then he whirled around and ran for the stairs, his robe billowing behind him in a greasy brown cloud. His hand flicked into his pocket. Yasmin glimpsed him throwing what looked like a small pocket watch and heard a familiar sound. *Tick, tick, tick.* There was a burst of smoke. The top of the lighthouse distorted like a fun-house mirror.

"Look out!" Yasmin shouted. "He's thrown a Time Crunch!"

The wood of the top stair began to warp and curl. Just like the apple in the Wrights' workshop, it was ageing and rotting before their eyes.

"Follow him!" Min-Jun shouted. He darted for the stairs.

"Cuckoo!" shouted Tempo in warning.

"It's too late, Min-Jun," Yasmin cried. "The stairs aren't safe!"

Min-Jun almost stumbled on the top step as it crumbled to dust. Yasmin pulled him back. The long, twisting spiral below them flaked and groaned, breaking into pieces – until with a resounding **CRACK** it fell away. There was nothing left but a high, yawning space. The Time Crunch had done its deadly work.

DeLay's mocking laughter floated up to them from the ground. "How are you going to get out of this one, hmm? There will be no powered flight today, tomorrow, or EVER. I'm going to enjoy watching those brothers go home as failures! Ha ha ha!"

Yasmin and Min-Jun rushed to the

edge of the platform on the lighthouse roof. DeLay was bounding away, his robe flying out behind him like a witch's cloak. His laughter rolled through their heads like the sound of the crashing waves on the shore.

Min-Jun beat his fist on the rail that encircled the platform they stood on. "I can't believe he got away!" he said, resting his head on his hands. "What are we going to do?"

Yasmin frowned at the skipping, flapping figure of the time villain as he raced away down the beach. "He doesn't

have the propeller anymore," she said. "It must be downstairs."

"Cuckoo!" agreed Tempo.

Min-Jun lifted his head. "So what? We can't get down to retrieve it, wherever he's put it."

Yasmin moved to the other side of the lighthouse. Way off in the distance, she could see the Wright brothers' hangar, and the bustle of activity around its wide, high doors. Orville and Wilbur were packing up their equipment, just as DeLay had predicted.

Yasmin couldn't imagine a world without aeroplanes. They had to figure out a way to fix this.

"Hey," she said suddenly. "Didn't Wilbur say something about using the lighthouse for some of their early flying experiments?"

"Yes…" Min-Jun said slowly.

Yasmin looked around. There was a lot of stuff lying about. Most of it was covered in dustsheets or propped up against the curved railings. Maybe there was something here that could help them.

She reached for the nearest dustsheet and tugged. It slithered to the floor, revealing a large roll of canvas. It was very like the material they had seen back in the workshop. In fact, it looked identical.

Yasmin moved to the next dustsheet. This one hid a box of thick sailors' needles and strong-looking thread. The next sheet revealed bundles of wooden struts. "Look at all this!" she said. "It might be just what we need. What's under that big dustsheet over there?"

Min-Jun dashed to the bulky, covered object. Yasmin joined him. Together, they pulled the sheet away. A battered glider

lay before them, made of wood and
canvas. It was dusty, and there were a few
holes in the canvas. One of the wings
looked a little crooked too. But it was big
enough to carry an adult – or two kids.

"Are you thinking what I'm
thinking?" Yasmin asked with excitement.

"Yes," said Min-Jun, "I think I am."

"We can use this to glide out of here!"
said Yasmin.

Min-Jun sighed. "We're
officially crazy."

"It just needs a bit of fixing up," said

Yasmin. "You're the modelling expert. Time to get modelling!"

She grabbed the box with the sailors' needles and thread and passed it to Min-Jun. He threaded a needle and started sewing up the holes in the glider's canvas wings.

Next, Yasmin took off her backpack and set it on the floor. After rummaging inside, she pulled out the strange weather vane object they had taken from the History Hub. She still hadn't worked the object out, but she knew it would be useful on their mission. The objects from the History Hub always were.

She stood it upright on the floor.

A strong gust of wind swirled the dust around her feet. Yasmin heard a clicking sound. The weather vane object was clicking gently, spinning where it stood.

Yasmin suddenly realised what it was.

"Anemometer!" she said.

"Bless you," said Min-Jun, threading one of the long sailors' needles with new thread.

Yasmin laughed. "The object we got from the History Hub – it's an anemometer. It measures wind!"

Min-Jun looked up. "So how does that help us?"

Yasmin studied the little object. The four sideways cups were spinning briskly now. "It tells us wind speed and direction," she said. "We can use it to judge the direction for launching the glider. There's no point taking off into a headwind. We'll just get blown back. We need a tailwind to push us along. And we need to know the wind speed so we can judge how to use the controls."

Min-Jun bit off his thread and tied a knot. He got to his feet and studied the glider wings. "This thing doesn't really have controls," he said. "Just a pulley system. Do you really think it'll fly?"

"Oh, it'll fly," said Yasmin with confidence. "This is the Wright brothers we're talking about. They worked out the

glider before they moved on to their powered flight ideas. Give me a piece of thread, will you?"

Min-Jun passed Yasmin a piece of the sturdy green yarn he had been using to mend the glider wings. Yasmin tied it to the stem of one of the cups. Using her Timekeepers watch, she measured the length of one of the rods that held the cups to the centre of the anemometer. "If I double this," she murmured, "I can calculate the diameter of the cups – that's the width – then multiply by pi, or roughly three, to find out the circumference – that's all the way round the circle…"

"You've totally lost me," said Min-Jun.

"I often have that effect," said Yasmin with a grin. She pressed the stopwatch feature on her watch, and timed the cups as they rotated for exactly one minute. "Right," she said, clicking the stopwatch. Using the maths she had learned from coding, she ran some swift calculations. "The wind is moving at approximately twenty miles an hour, and coming from the east. If we launch the glider here" – she patted the railing beside her – "then we have the best chance of catching that wind and gliding down to the beach."

"And you can tell all that from those little cups?" said Min-Jun in astonishment.

Yasmin tapped her nose. "Four little cups and some mathematics," she said.

"Cuckoo!" said Tempo, a little anxiously.

The theory was good. But would it work in practice? There was only one way to find out!

Chapter 7

Take off!

Yasmin and Min-Jun took up their
positions, standing up between the glider's
wings. Min-Jun held on with both hands.
Yasmin held on with just one. Her other
hand clutched the anemometer.

"Wait until there's a decent gust of
wind," she warned.

"I'm going nowhere until you say so,"
said Min-Jun. He looked a little pale. The
ground was a long way off.

There was a sudden gust. The
anemometer cups spun vigorously.

"NOW!" shouted Yasmin.

They ran forward, holding on tightly.
As they reached the railings around the
top of the lighthouse, they both jumped,
tucked their legs underneath them and
landed flat on their tummies on
the glider.

There was a lurch as the glider
dropped over the edge. For one horrible
moment, they plunged downwards –
until, with a bounce, the wind caught the
underside of the glider's wings and they
levelled out. They'd done it! They
were flying!

"Whoo!" shouted Yasmin.

"Yeah!" roared Min-Jun.

The wind tore at their hair and lashed at their clothes. Yasmin felt like she was catching a ride on an enormous bird.

"Cuckoo!" shouted Tempo happily, flapping her wings beside Yasmin's head as she did her best to keep up with the glider. "Cuckoo!"

Yasmin had judged the wind direction just right. The nose of the glider began to dip, lower and lower, until the wooden runners beneath met the soft sand of the beach. They skidded down the beach, drifting from side to side, until at last – they stopped.

Yasmin threw her arms in the air, giddy with the thrill of the flight. "That was AMAZING!" she shouted.

Min-Jun grinned weakly as he slid off the glider. "Amazing is one way of putting it," he said.

They had landed a short distance from the lighthouse. Yasmin ran back towards the warped wooden door, and the curved wall where their bicycles still stood. She raced inside, hoping DeLay hadn't broken the propeller out of spite.

No! It was still there!

Yasmin took one end. Min-Jun took the other. They carefully carried the propeller outside, and balanced it on the handlebars of the two bicycles, just as they had earlier. Then they wheeled the bicycles back up to the boardwalk and pushed them towards the hangar.

"We need to go faster," Yasmin urged Min-Jun. "I don't want DeLay showing up again and throwing another Time Crunch."

"I'm going as fast as I can!" Min-Jun exclaimed.

It took them fifteen minutes of fast walking and pushing before they reached the hangar. Wilbur and Orville both came running out to meet them.

"You found it!" Orville gasped.

Wilbur did a little happy dance in front of the hangar. "I can't believe it!" he said. "We thought everything was lost and that DeLay guy had won!"

"We had almost packed up the whole workshop," Orville admitted.

Yasmin patted the propeller. "You can still make your flight happen," she said.

Orville grinned broadly. "You're right," he said. "We haven't come this far to give up now."

"You've really inspired us!" said

Wilbur. "If this flight goes to plan, well…
who knows how far humans will be able
to fly one day?"

"Maybe as far as the next town!"
said Orville.

Yasmin and Min-Jun shared a
knowing grin. "Maybe," said
Yasmin, laughing.

Word spread through the small settlement of Kitty Hawk that the Wright brothers were making another attempt to fly their machine down the beach. As the sound of hammering filled the hangar, with Orville and Wilbur reattaching the propeller and Yasmin and Min-Jun helping with a few last-minute adjustments to the Flyer, people started drifting into view. Some came in groups. One or two came alone. Straw hats flapped in the strong winter breeze. Scarves flew like woollen flags around people's necks, and skirts whipped and snapped around the ladies' legs. There was a sense of anticipation in the air. Tempo sat high up on the top of the hangar, squawking happily.

"I think we're ready," said Wilbur, straightening up from where he had been tightening one of the wires that crisscrossed between the slim wooden struts and held the wings in place. "Just need to check the wind speed. Hey, Orville! Where's the anemometer?"

"I don't know," said Orville, scratching his head. "Maybe we packed it away?"

The brothers looked dismayed.

They needed to know the wind speed and direction or the flight couldn't take place. They couldn't fail now!

"Use ours," Yasmin offered. And she pulled the History Hub anemometer from her bag.

Wilbur looked incredulous. "Where would we be without you two?" he said, shaking his head.

The wind speed had picked up, and was now twenty-seven miles per hour.

"It's a little fast," Wilbur admitted. "But we'll give it our best shot. Hey Orville, want to toss for who gets to be the pilot?"

The brothers tossed a small silver coin. Orville won. Ramming his leather helmet on his head, Orville grinned and climbed aboard. He settled into position, lying down on his front.

"You two better get into the crowd if you want a decent view," said Wilbur. "I think we're about to make history!"

Chapter 8

First flight

Yasmin felt a flutter of excitement as she and Min-Jun joined the crowds down on the beach. The numbers had swelled as word had spread of this latest attempt to conquer the sky. Was this it? Was this the moment? Someone started playing a barrel organ. Someone else had started

selling ices. There was a carnival
atmosphere as the residents of Kitty
Hawk prepared to watch
something astonishing.

Yasmin heard the throaty roar of an
engine. The nose of the Flyer appeared.
Then the rest of the machine. The
runners lifted off the ground. The whole
machine drove forward into nothing.
And… lift off!

"Ooh!" cried the crowd. "Aaah!"

Yasmin watched as the Flyer zoomed over her head. She was dimly aware of a man with a camera on legs beside her, bending down and – **SNAP!** – taking a photograph of the moment so that it would be captured for all time. Five seconds in the air…then ten…

The Flyer gently dipped down and skidded to a halt on the sand some way down the beach. It had been airborne for a full twelve seconds. Orville Wright had just made the first powered flight the world had ever seen.

The crowd erupted. Hats were thrown into the air. Scarves were waved like banners. What a moment! Yasmin breathed it in. She turned to Min-Jun.

"Mission accomplished," she said
with satisfaction.

He nodded with a wide smile.
It was time to go.

The children slipped away quietly
from the celebrating crowd, and made
their way around the side of the hangar.
It wouldn't be good for the people of
Kitty Hawk to see them vanish into
thin air. It would have been one miracle
too many.

DeLay was waiting for them,
scowling. His white hair blew
around his head as he stabbed
the air with a long
bony finger.

"You might have put history back on track this time, but this isn't the last you've seen of me," he threatened. "I'll be back. And next time, I'll succeed!"

Min-Jun folded his arms. "We're not scared of you, DeLay," he said.

"Whatever you throw at the Timekeepers, we'll be ready!" Yasmin added.

DeLay gave a sly grin. "That's what YOU think. I have time to get it right one day. Plenty of time…HA!"

There was a flash of fire, a cloud of smoke, and the clattering sound of chiming clocks.

Then he vanished, as if he'd never been there at all.

"Cuckoo!" Tempo fluttered down from her perch on the hangar. She zoomed around Min-Jun and Yasmin, round and round in a blur of brown stripes, until Yasmin felt quite dizzy. Everything went white…

Yasmin felt her feet touch down on the familiar stone floor of the History Hub. Beside her, Min-Jun dusted himself down and offered Yasmin a high five.

"Cuckoo!" cried Tempo in celebration.

The other Timekeepers ran over.

"Well done!" cried Rosa, patting them both on the back. Dry mud spattered onto the stone floor. "Oops," she added, staring at her muddy hands.

"We knew you'd succeeded," said Hannah with a grin. "We have evidence. Want to see?"

Yasmin spotted a postcard on the History Hub wall. It showed a girl in a long dress and a straw hat, and a boy in a checked woollen hat, standing on the edge of a photograph showing the Flyer in mid-air. Yasmin and Min-Jun had been caught by the photographer at Kitty Hawk! Yasmin's heart soared.

"We couldn't have done it without your help, guys," said Min-Jun.

The history of aviation had been well and truly saved.

It was time for everyone to get back to their everyday lives. The Timekeepers waved each other goodbye, with more cheering and celebration and back-patting.

Yasmin hugged Min-Jun. "Thanks for the needlework, partner," she joked.

Min-Jun laughed. "Thanks for the maths! See you next time!"

Yasmin pressed a button on her watch. There was a rainbow flash of light and a sense of flying that reminded her of the glider, before she felt herself touch down. For a moment, she felt as if she was back in Kitty Hawk – because she had arrived back beside the replica of the Flyer. No time had passed at all. But she grinned when she saw the old photograph on the display panel. There she was, standing beside Min-Jun as the Flyer took off. It was the photograph from the History Hub.

"Come on, Yasmin!" her dad called. "The air display is about to begin!"

Yasmin ran out of the hangar with

her parents. There was a huge **BOOM** –
and a line of jets powered overhead,
angling their sleek wings to catch the
bright Karachi sun. Plumes of coloured
smoke trailed behind them in smart lines
and patterns, crisscrossing the blue sky.

Yasmin smiled privately to herself. To
think, she'd been there when it all began!

Yasmin's
TIMEKEEPER JOURNAL

Wilbur, Orville, and Katharine Wright were siblings from Ohio, USA. While history remembers the two brothers as the pioneers of flight, Katharine was also a key member of the dynamic team.

Wilbur Wright (1867–1912)

Wilbur was a keen inventor from an early age, but also loved sports. An injury stopped him from attending college as an athlete, so he started a business with Orville.

Did you know?
The brothers tossed a coin to see who would fly first, and Orville won.

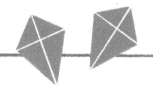

Orville Wright (1871–1948)

Orville loved flying kites as a child, which may have inspired his love of aviation. He also enjoyed cycling, and along with his siblings, opened a bicycle shop. Their experiments here eventually lead to designs for an aircraft.

Katharine Wright (1874–1929)

After spending time as a teacher, Katharine Wright ran the Wright's bicycle shop when her brothers focussed on planes. She was also the main contact for her brothers' business dealings, and organized the media events around their flights.

The Wright
FLYER

After many experiments and attempts, the Wright brothers successfully made the first human-powered flight on December 17, 1903 in an aircraft called the Wright Flyer.

Rudder for steering

Propeller to move the plane forward

12 m (40 ft) wingspan

The first flight only lasted 12 seconds, but within a few years, a version of the flyer could stay in the air for almost 40 minutes!

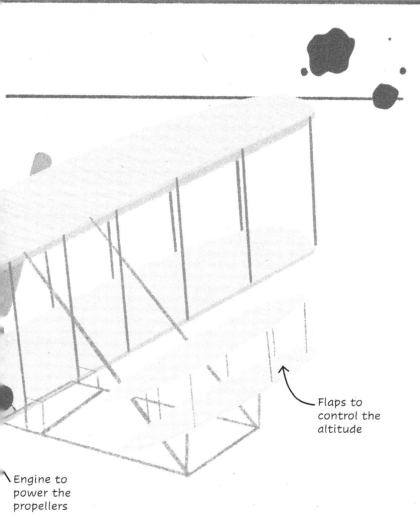

Flaps to
control the
altitude

Engine to
power the
propellers

Fly like a bird
The Wright brothers studied
birds in flight and were inspired
by the movement of their
wings. This influenced
the design of their plane.

Timeline of *FLIGHT*

Throughout history, there has always been a desire to fly. Over time, what started as a dream became reality, as these inventions and milestones allowed humans to experience flight in new and exciting ways.

First hot air balloon flight
French inventors Joseph-Michel and Jacques-Etienne Montgolfier built a balloon from linen, and sailed over Paris for 25 minutes.

1903

1852

1783

First powered, controlled flight
The Wright brothers flew for 12 seconds and covered around 30 m (120 ft).

First powered and steered airship
French engineer Henri Giffard's steam-powered airship flew almost 27km (17 miles) through France at a speed of around 10 kph (6 mph).

First commercial flight

The world's first regularly scheduled heavier-than-air flight took off from Florida, USA on New Year's Day, 1914.

First flight around the world

A team from the US Army Air Service flew for more than 175 days, landing in 22 different countries along the way.

First human in space

Russian-born Yuri Gagarin became the first person to travel into space, orbiting the Earth for 108 minutes.

1914

1919

1924

1947

1961

First transatlantic flight

British pilots Captain Alcock and Lieutenant Whitten Brown became the first people to fly non-stop across the Atlantic Ocean.

Breaking the speed of sound

U.S. Air Force Captain Chuck Yeager flew faster than the speed of sound, which is 1,234 kph (767 mph).

Quiz

1: What were the names of the two Wright brothers?

2: True or false: The Wright brothers had a sister named Katherine.

3: What device does DeLay use to slow or speed up time?

4: True or false: The Wright brothers made the first human powered flight in the year 1903.

5: What object does DeLay steal from the Wright brothers?

6: What type of bird is Tempo?

7: True or false: The Wright brothers' plane was called *The Skybird*.

Glossary

Anemometer
A tool used to measure the speed of the wind.

Camouflage
Colours or patterns that help things blend in with their environment.

Canvas
A strong cloth that is often used to make sails or tents.

Dune
Small mounds or ridges of sand formed by the wind or flowing water.

Dustsheet
A piece of cloth used to cover and protect things from dust or paint.

Flight simulator

A machine that re-creates the conditions of flight, often used to train pilots.

Gears

A machine part used to increase force or speed.

Glider

A type of aircraft that flies without an engine.

Hangar

A large building where aircraft are stored.

Karachi

A large city in Pakistan.

Pendulum

A weight suspended on a stick or rope, often used in clocks.

Propeller

A mechanical device found in planes or boats that helps create movement.

Plume

A cloud of smoke or dust that looks like a feather.

Rudder

The part of a ship or aircraft that is used to help steer

Spitfire

A British fighter plane used during World War II

Strut

A bar, rod, or brace that helps support a structure.

Time crunch

A magic device used by DeLay to control the flow of time.

Time travel

The ability to travel back and forward in time to visit the past or future.

Wrench

A tool used to tighten or loosen something.

Quiz Answers

1. Orville and Wilbur
2. True
3. Time Crunches
4. True
5. A propeller
6. A cuckoo
7. False – it was the *Wright Flyer*

DK | Penguin Random House

For my father and grandfather, pilots of the past.

Text for DK by Working Partners Ltd
9 Kingsway, London WC2B 6XF
With special thanks to Lucy Courtenay

Design by Collaborate Ltd
Illustrator Esther Hernando
Consultant Anita Ganeri
Acquisitions Editor James Mitchem
Editors Becca Arlington, Abi Maxwell
Designers Ann Cannings, Rachael Prokic, Elle Ward
Jacket and Sales Material Coordinator Magda Pszuk
Senior Production Editor Dragana Puvavic
Production Controller Leanne Burke
Publishing Director Sarah Larter

First published in Great Britain in 2023 by
Dorling Kindersley Limited
One Embassy Gardens, 8 Viaduct Gardens,
London, SW11 7AY

A CIP catalogue record for this book
is available from the British Library.
ISBN: 978-0-2415-3865-4

Printed and bound in Great Britain by
Clays Ltd, Elcograf S.p.A.

For the curious
www.dk.com

The publisher would like to thank Lynne Murray for picture library assistance.